DUCK in the TRUCK

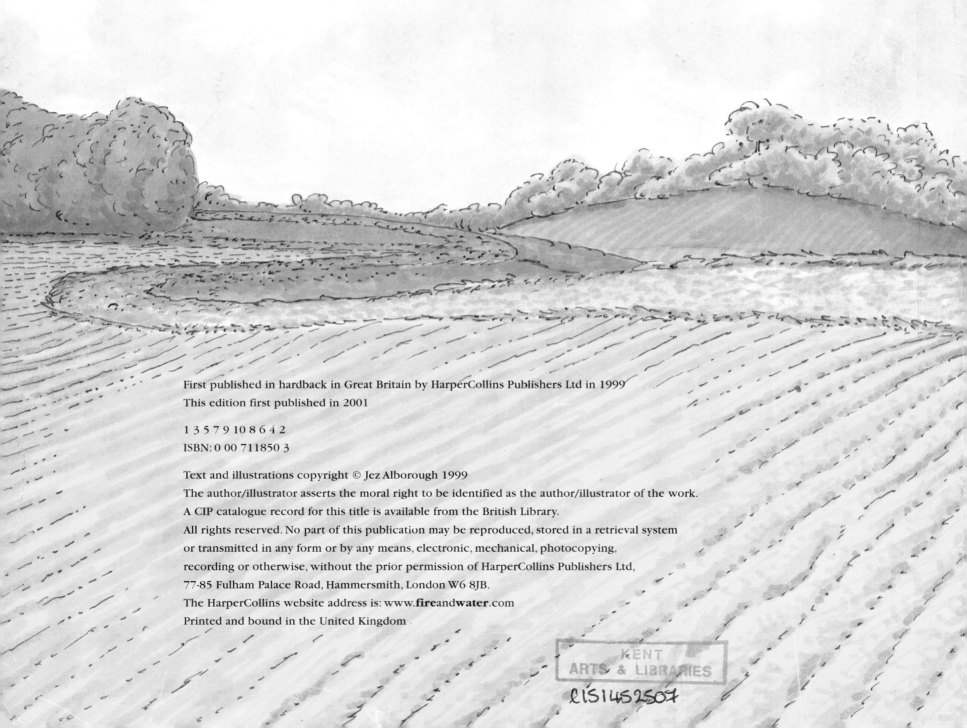

For Gail

First published in hardback in Great Britain by HarperCollins Publishers Ltd in 1999
This edition first published in 2001

1 3 5 7 9 10 8 6 4 2
ISBN: 0 00 711850 3

DUCK in the TRUCK

Jez Alborough

Collins

An Imprint of HarperCollinsPublishers

This is the Duck driving home in a truck.

This is the track which is taking him back.

This is the rock struck by the truck   and this is

muck   where the truck becomes stuck.

These are the feet which
jump the Duck down

into the muck
all yucky and brown.

This is the frog who
spies from the bush

and croaks "I'll help you
give it a push!"

This is the push of a Frog   and a Duck...

And this is the truck still stuck.

This is a sheep
driving home in a jeep.

"Get out of the way,"
he yells with a beep.

This is the quack of an angry Duck.
"I can't," he snaps "my truck is stuck."

This is the
quiet…

...as they think
what to do.

"Got it !" croaks Frog,
"Sheep can push too."

This is the slurp   and squelch   and suck

as the Sheep steps slowly through the muck.

This is the push of a Sheep, a Frog   and a Duck

and this is the truck… still stuck.

This is the happy sleepy goat relaxing on his motorboat.

This is the ear that
hears the shout,

"My truck's in the muck
and it won't come out!"

This is the rope
and here's the Goat's plan,

to tie a knot
as tight as they can.

This is the push at the rear once again.

This is the pull as the boat takes the strain.

These are
the wheels

finally
gripping

this is
the knot

TWANG

suddenly
slipping

This is the truck with the engine on fast

back on the track… UNSTUCK AT LAST!

This is the Duck driving home in the truck

leaving the Frog, the Sheep and the Goat...

STUCK IN THE MUCK!